This book belongs to:

....

....

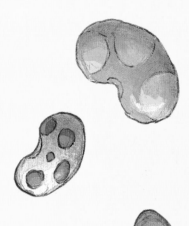

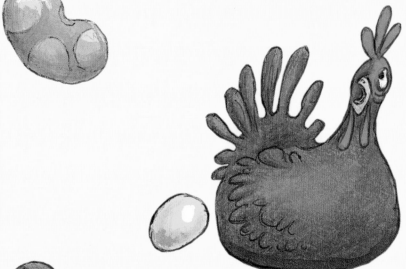

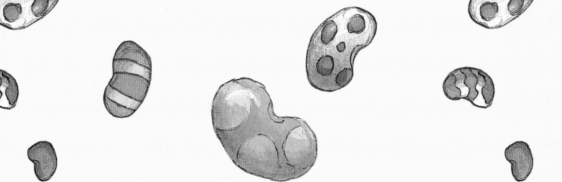

Retold by Sue Graves
Illustrated by Andy Catling

Reading consultants: Betty Root and Monica Hughes

This edition published by Parragon in 2011

Parragon
Queen Street House
4 Queen Street
Bath BA1 1HE, UK

ISBN 978-1-4454-3601-2

Printed in China

Jack and the Beanstalk

Bath • New York • Singapore • Hong Kong • Cologne • Delhi
Melbourne • Amsterdam • Johannesburg • Auckland • Shenzhen

Helping your child to read

These books are closely linked to recognized learning strategies. Their vocabulary has been carefully selected from word lists recommended by educational experts.

Read the story
Read the story to your child a few times.

Follow your finger
Run your finger under the text as you read. Soon your child will begin to follow the words with you.

Once upon a time there was a boy called Jack.
He lived with his mother in a cottage.
They were very poor.
One day, Jack's mother said, "Take the cow to market and sell her."
So Jack took the cow to market.

8

Look at the pictures
Talk about the pictures. They will help your child to understand the story.

Jack took the cow to market.

9

Give it a try
Let your child try reading the large type on each right-hand page. It repeats a line from the story.

Join in
When your child is ready, encourage him or her to join in with the main story text. Shared reading is the first step to reading alone.

Once upon a time there was a boy
called Jack.
He lived with his mother in a cottage.
They were very poor.
One day, Jack's mother said, "Take the
cow to market and sell her."
So Jack took the cow to market.

Jack took the cow to market.

On the way, Jack met an old man.
"Where are you going?" asked the
old man.
"I am going to market to sell the cow,"
said Jack.
"Will you sell the cow for five magic
beans?" said the old man.
So Jack sold the cow for five beans.

Jack sold the cow for five beans.

Jack took the beans home.
"I sold the cow for five magic beans,"
he said.
"Five beans!" said Jack's mother.
She was angry.
She threw the beans out the window.
Then she sent Jack to bed.

She threw the beans out
the window.

In the morning, Jack woke up.
He looked out the window.
There was a giant beanstalk.
It went up, up into the sky.
Jack climbed up the beanstalk.

14

There was a giant beanstalk.

At last Jack got to the top of the
beanstalk.

He saw a giant castle.

Jack knocked on the door.

The door opened.

Jack went in.

He saw a giant castle.

In the castle lived a giant and his wife.
"Fee, fi, fo, fum!" said the giant.
"I want my breakfast!"
Jack was scared.
"You must hide," said the giant's wife,
"or the giant will eat you."

"Fee, fi, fo, fum!"

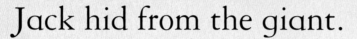
Jack hid from the giant.
The giant sat down at the table.
Then he put a hen on the table.
"Hen, lay an egg!" said the giant.
"Cluck!" said the hen.
And the hen laid a golden egg.

The hen laid a golden egg.

"Here is your breakfast," said the
giant's wife.

His wife gave him a very big breakfast!

The giant ate his very big breakfast.

Then the giant felt very sleepy.

"Time for my nap," he said.

Soon he was fast asleep.

22

The giant felt very sleepy.

"A golden egg!" said Jack. "I will take the hen. She will make us rich."
The giant was fast asleep.
So Jack took the hen.
"Cluck!" said the hen.
The giant woke up!
Jack ran. The giant ran after him.

Jack took the hen.

But Jack got his ax.
He chopped down the beanstalk.
The giant fell down.
And that was the end of him.
Then the hen laid a golden egg.
So Jack and his mother were rich.

The giant fell down.

Look back in your book.
Can you read these words?

Jack

giant

cow

hen

beans

egg

Can you answer these questions?

How many magic beans
did Jack have?

What did the giant say?

What did the hen lay?

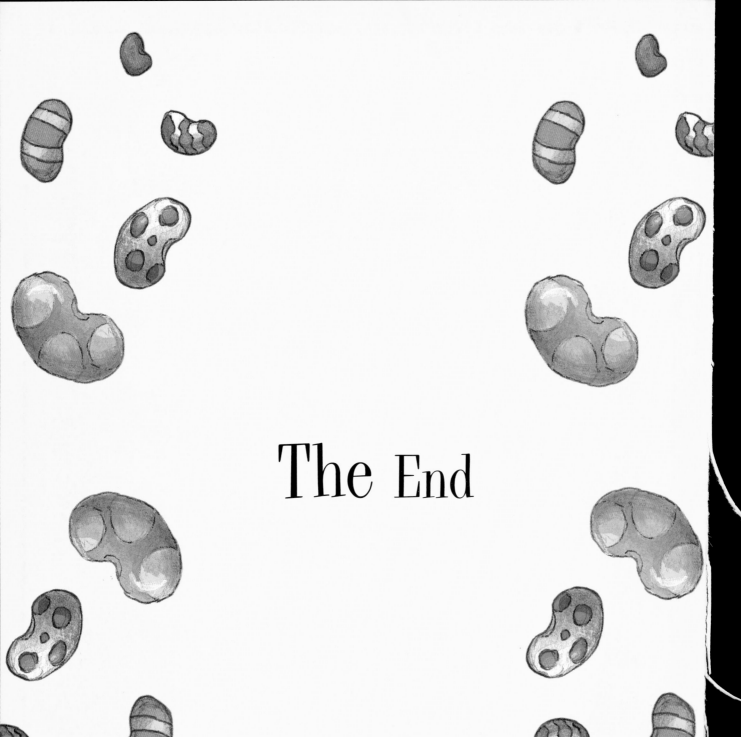

The End